LEGEND OF THE KING
KIOS CHRONICLES
VOLUME 1

Special Thanks!

I WANT TO TAKE THIS SPACE TO SAY THANK YOU, TO YOU, THE READER. YOU WERE ADVENTUROUS ENOUGH TO BUY A COMIC FROM A NEW, UNKNOWN COMIC CREATOR. I TRULY HOPE YOU ENJOY LEGEND OF THE KING, BECAUSE I ENJOYED MAKING IT FOR YOU. AND WITHOUT YOU THERE IS NO REAL REASON TO MAKE COMICS. SO, SINCERELY, THANK YOU!

Adam Stoak

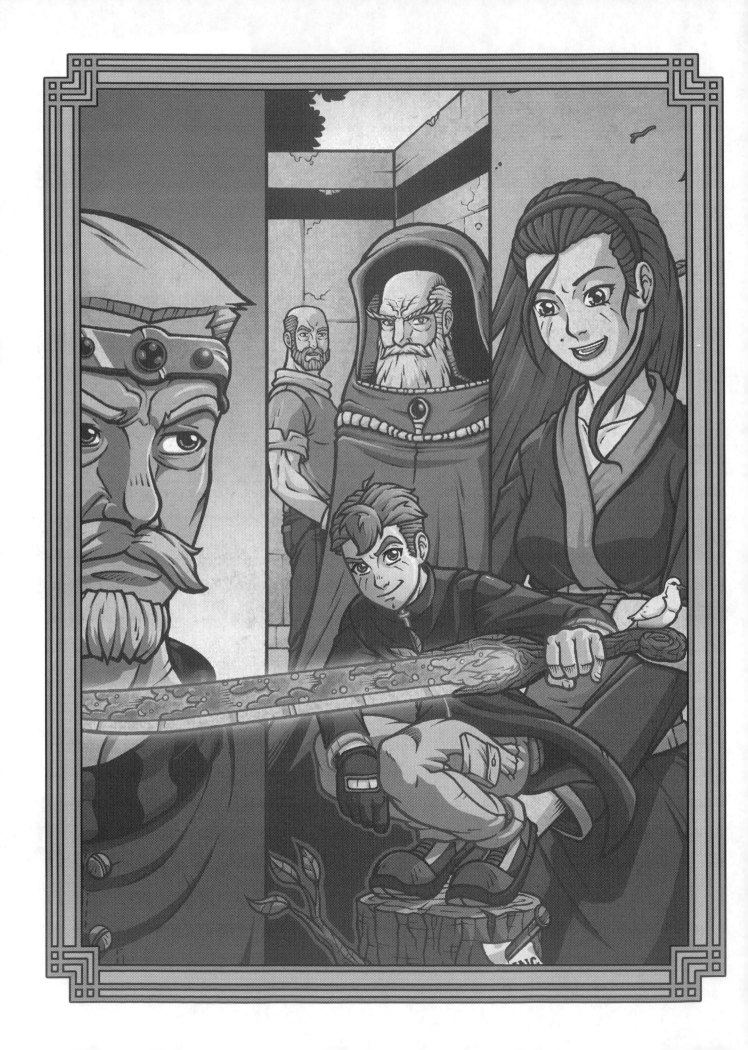

LEGEND OF THE KING
KIOS CHRONICLES

Created by

ADAM STOAK

Edited in Part by

JENN NOLL
BILL GREENE
KELLY STOAK

WestBow Press books may be ordered through booksellers or by contacting:

WestBow Press
A Division of Thomas Nelson
1663 Liberty Drive
Bloomington, IN 47403
www.westbowpress.com
1 (866) 928-1240

Because of the dynamic nature of the Internet, any web addresses or links contained in this book may have changed since publication and may no longer be valid. The views expressed in this work are solely those of the author and do not necessarily reflect the views of the publisher, and the publisher hereby disclaims any responsibility for them.

Any people depicted in stock imagery provided by Thinkstock are models, and such images are being used for illustrative purposes only.
Certain stock imagery © Thinkstock.

ISBN: 978-1-4497-6284-1 (sc)
ISBN: 978-1-4908-3826-7 (e)

Library of Congress Control Number: 2012914289

Printed in the United States of America.

WestBow Press rev. date: 05/20/2014

FOR MY BEAUTIFUL KAVALIE
QUEEN KELLY, AND OUR TWO
LITTLE FLAME USERS
SIMON AND KOLE.

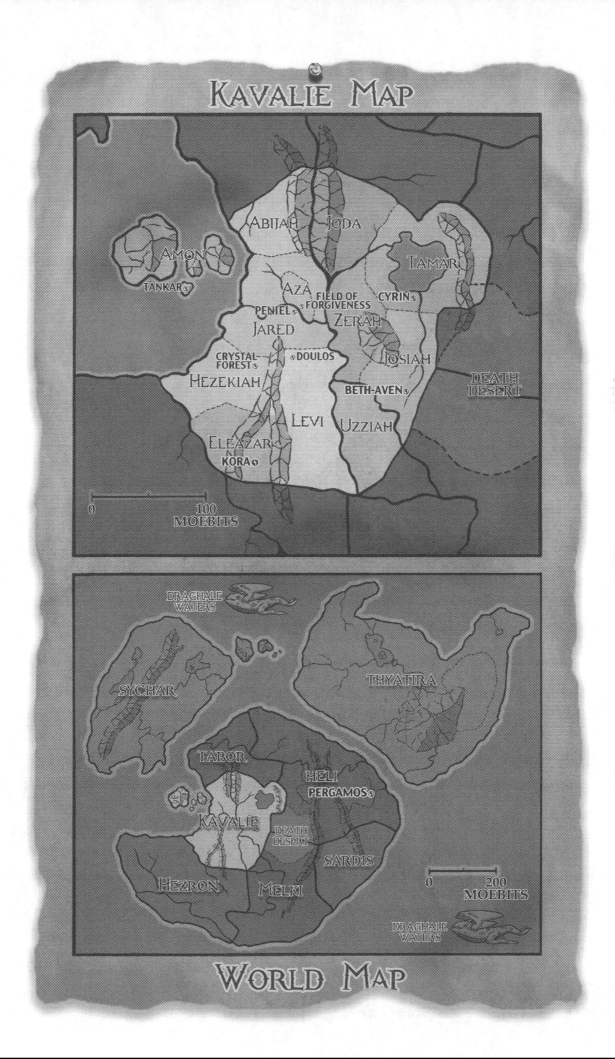

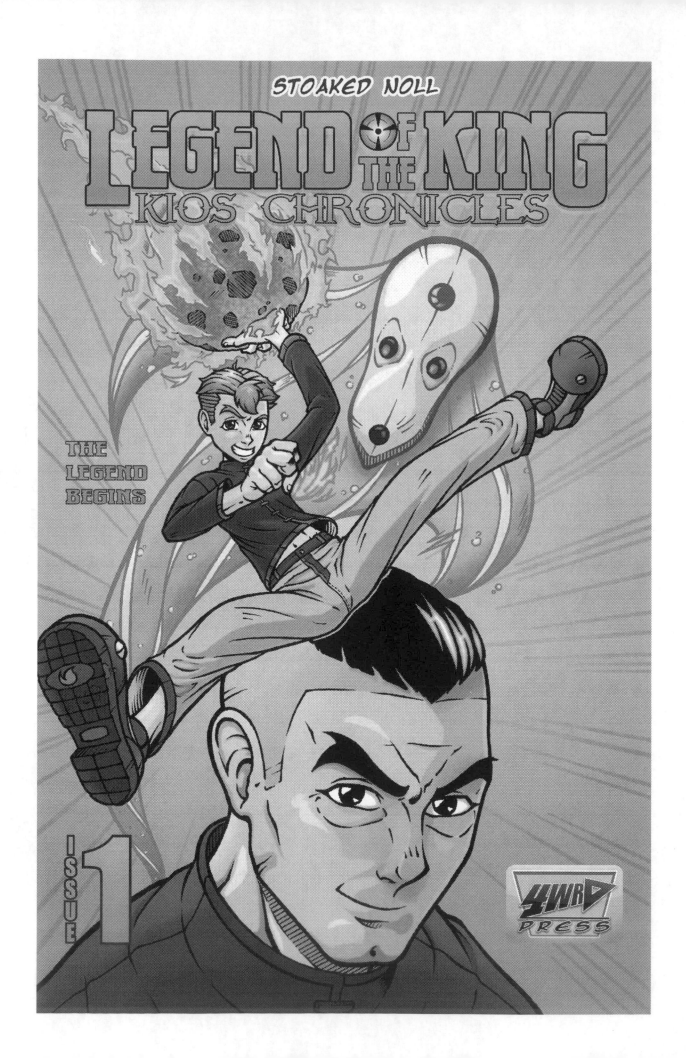

*RYU MEANS STYLE OR TECHNIQUE

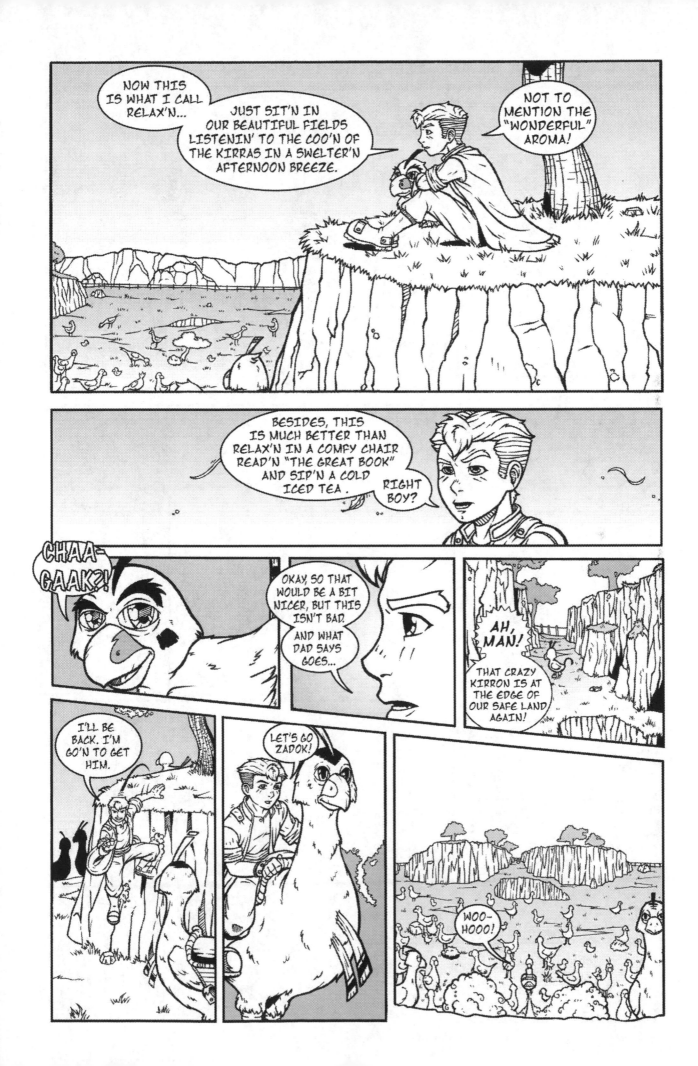

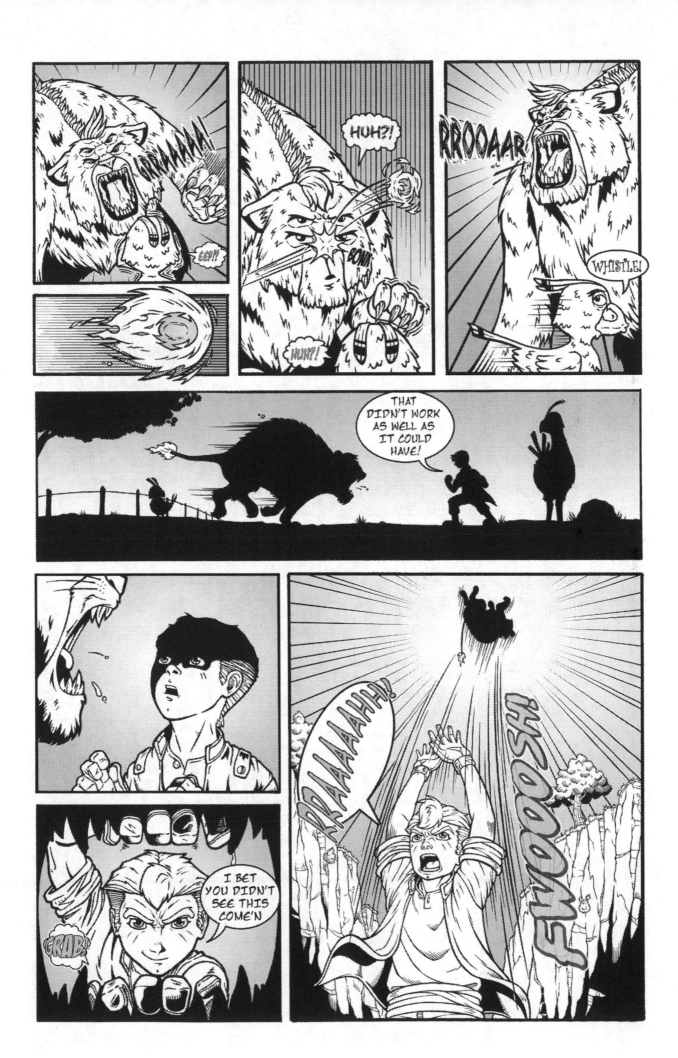

THE CHRONICLES CONTINUE IN ISSUE 2!

KIOS ON THE ROAD SOMEWHERE BETWEEN BETH-AVEN AND PENIEL.

SIR, DO YOU KNOW WHAT I'LL BE DO'N FOR THE KING?

IT'S MARCUS. YEAH, YOU'LL PROBABLY RUN ERRANDS JUST LIKE ALL HIS OTHER SERVANTS.

DO YOU KNOW, IS THE KING NICE?

HE USED TO BE, BUT NOT SO MUCH ANYMORE. STILL, YOU'LL BE OKAY. THERE'S SOMETHING SPECIAL ABOUT YOU! I MEAN, YOU DID DEFEAT A BION ALL BY YOURSELF!

*ONE MOEBIT IS EQUAL TO ABOUT 1 1/4 MILES.

THE CHRONICLES CONTINUE IN ISSUE 3

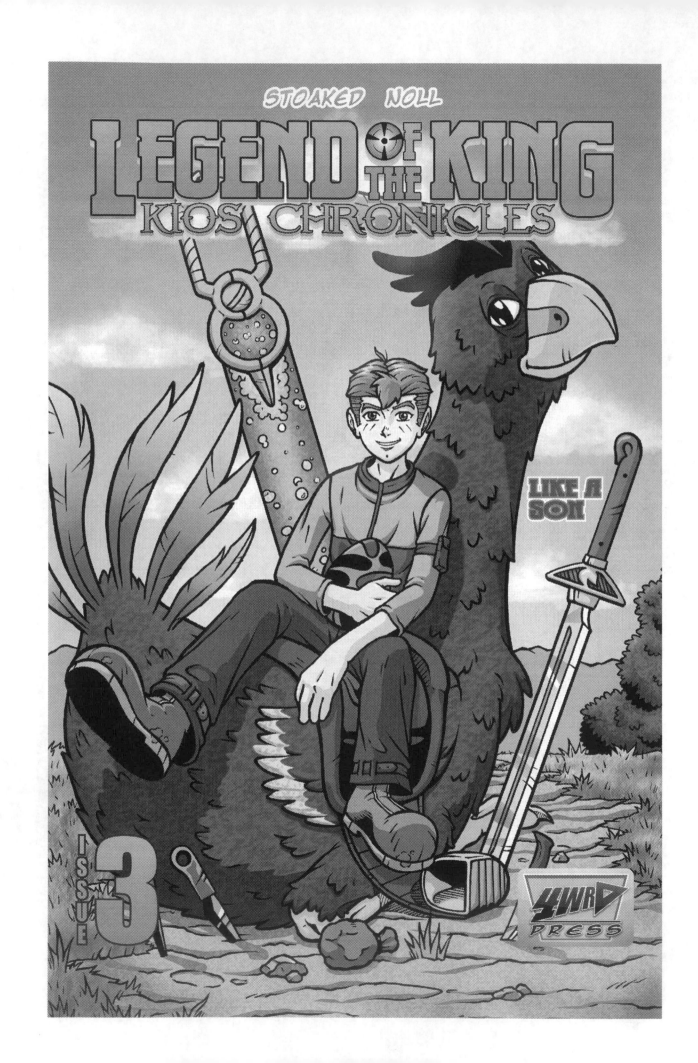

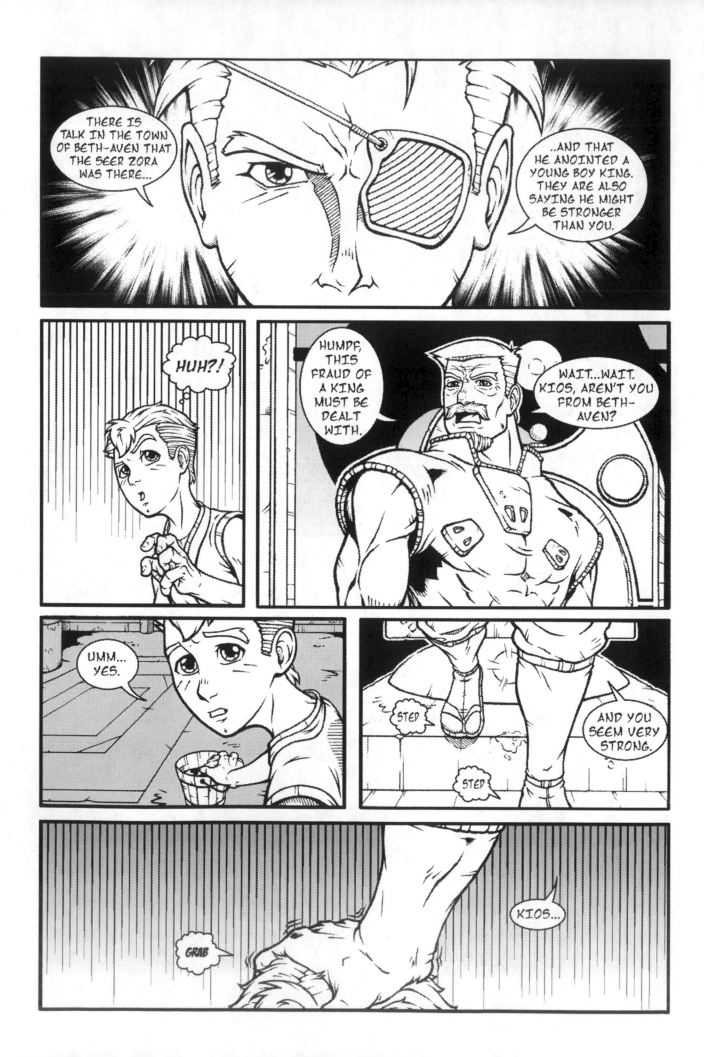

THE CHRONICLES CONTINUE IN ISSUE 4

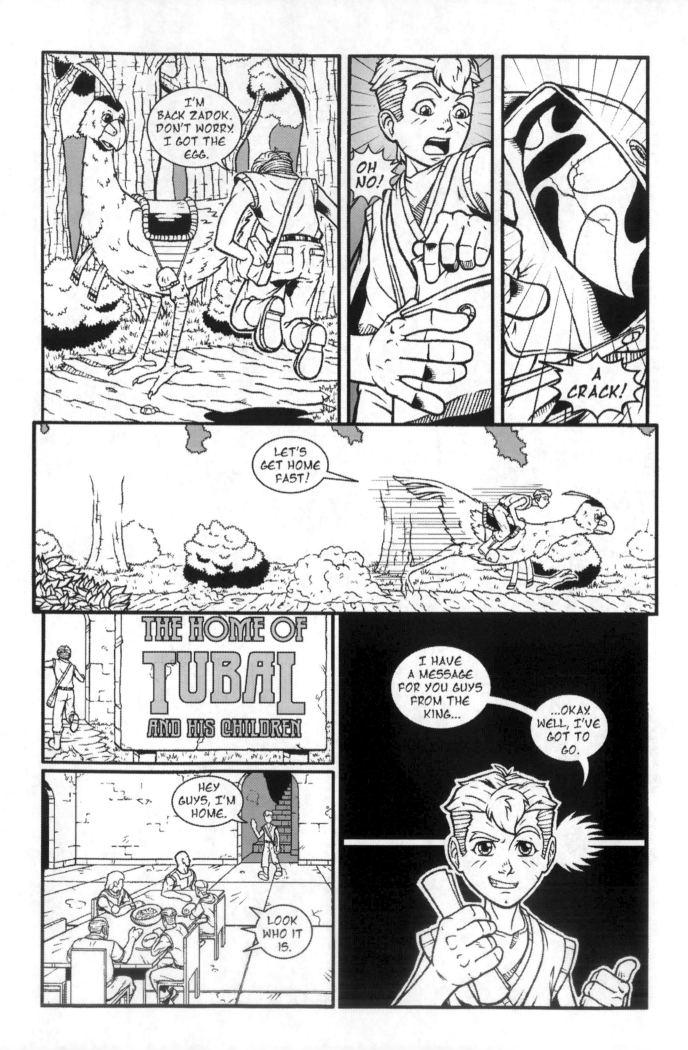

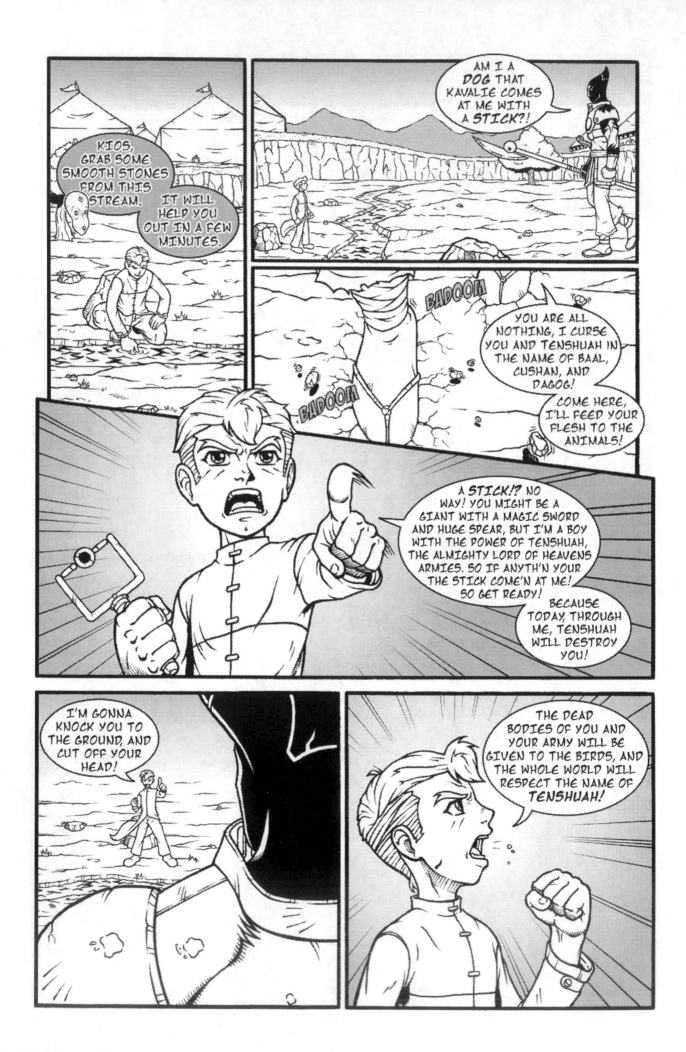

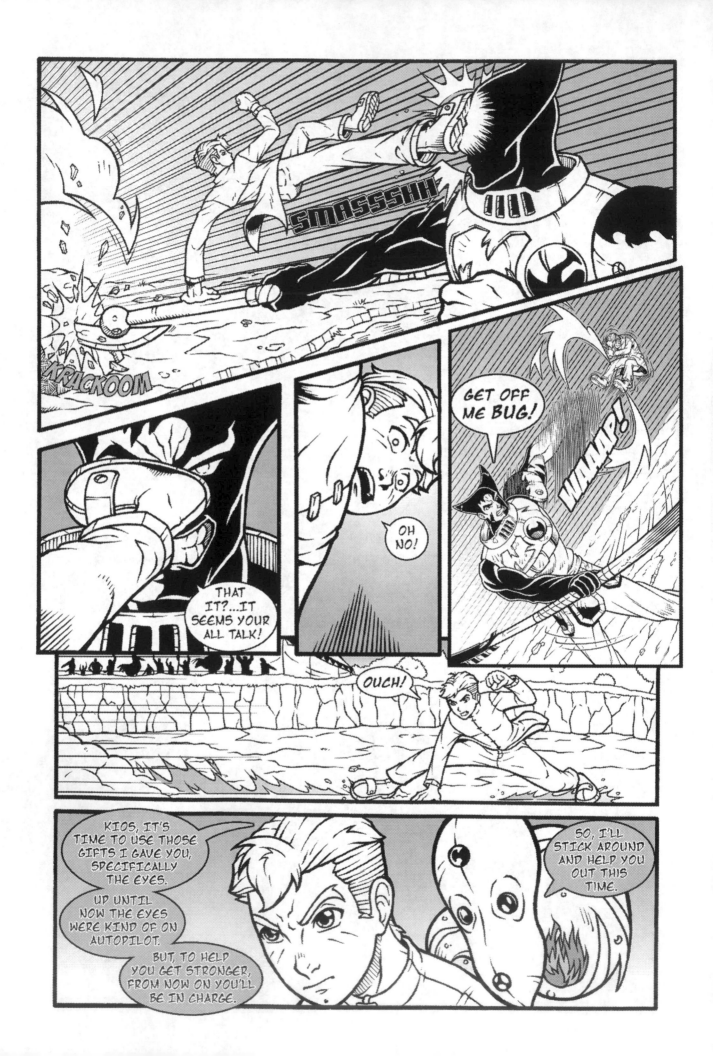

...SPIRIT SWORD!
WOW... THAT'S A... PRETTY COOL TWIG!
YOU THERE. SOLDIER.
YES, SIRE.
I WANT TO INFORM YOU OF SOMETHING!

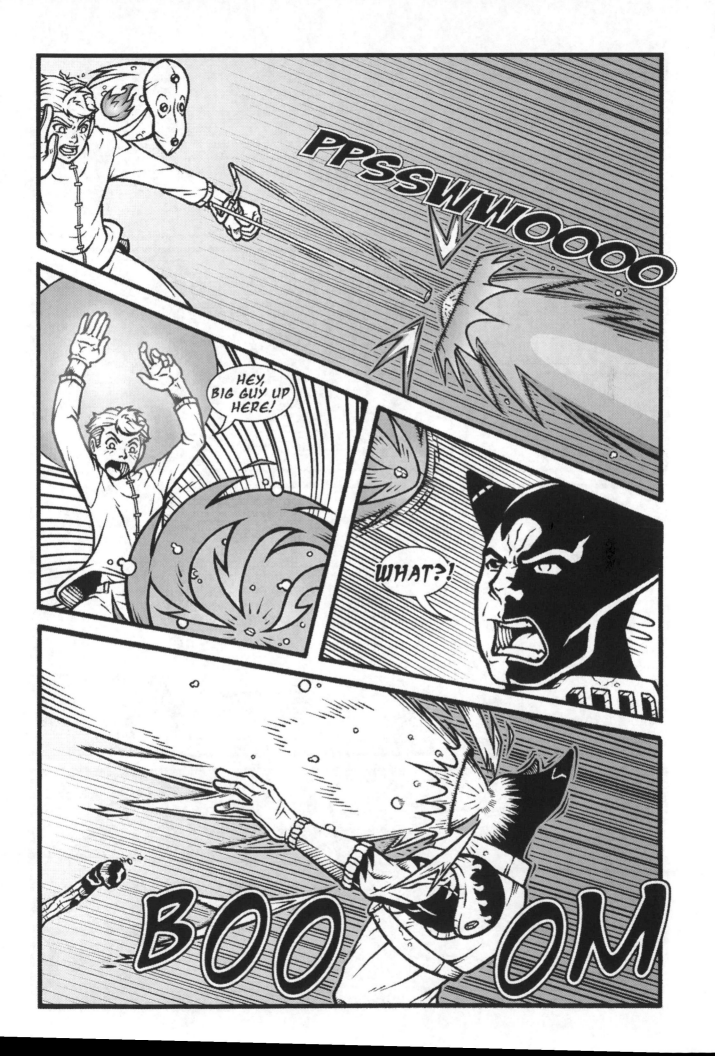

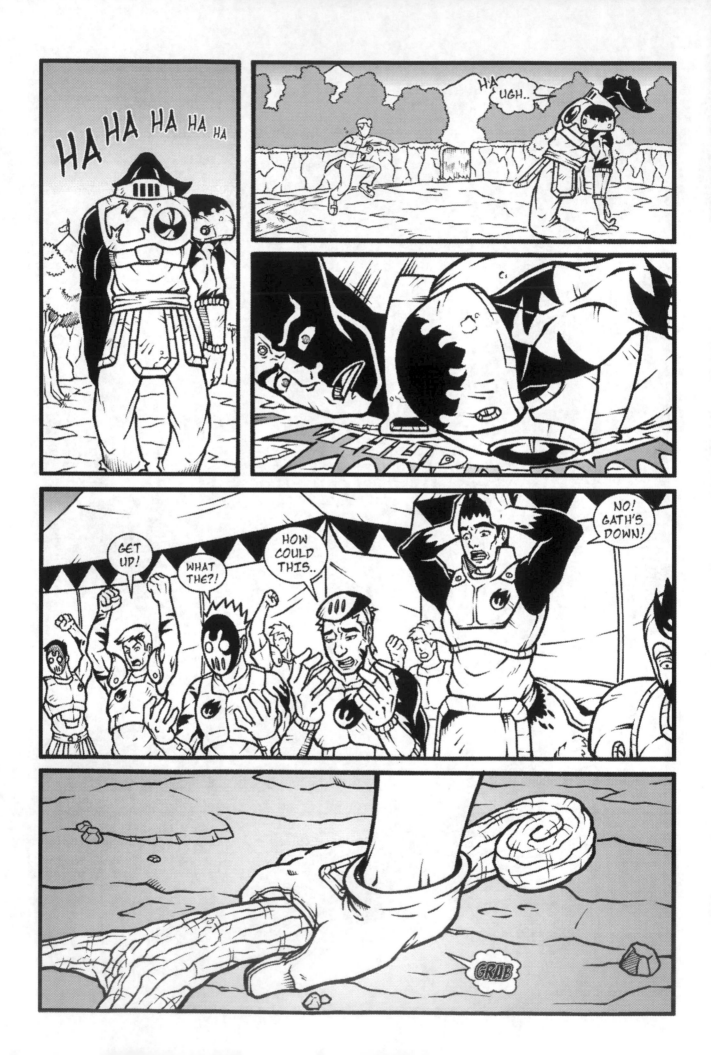

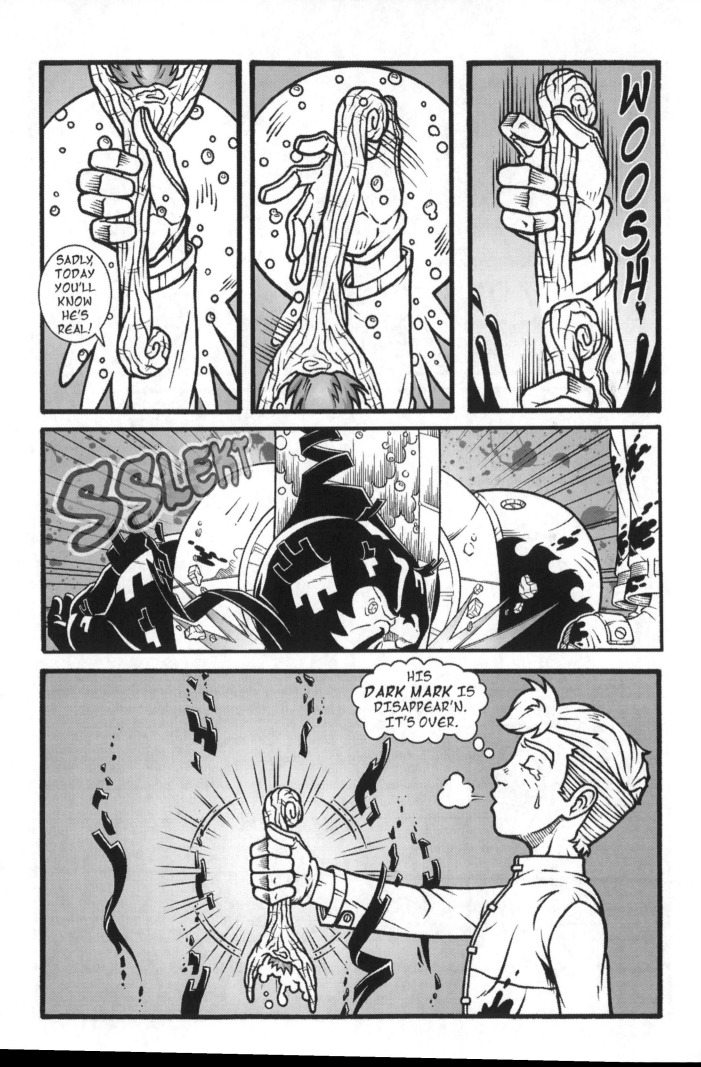

A SONG OF KIOS.

BEND DOWN, O TENSHUAH, AND HEAR MY PRAYER;
   ANSWER ME, FOR I NEED YOUR HELP.
PROTECT ME, FOR I AM DEVOTED TO YOU.
   SAVE ME, FOR I SERVE YOU AND TRUST YOU.
   YOU ARE MY SOVEREIGN KING.
BE MERCIFUL TO ME, O TENSHUAH,
   FOR I AM CALLING ON YOU CONSTANTLY.
GIVE ME HAPPINESS, O TENSHUAH,
   FOR I GIVE MYSELF TO YOU.
O TENSHUAH, YOU ARE SO GOOD, SO READY TO FORGIVE,
   SO FULL OF UNFAILING LOVE FOR ALL WHO ASK FOR
   YOUR HELP.
LISTEN CLOSELY TO MY PRAYER, O TENSHUAH;
   HEAR MY URGENT CRY.
I WILL CALL TO YOU WHENEVER I'M IN TROUBLE,
   AND YOU WILL ANSWER ME.

NO DARK NATION GOD IS LIKE YOU, O TENSHUAH.
   NONE CAN DO WHAT YOU DO!
ALL THE NATIONS YOU MADE
   WILL COME AND BOW BEFORE YOU, TENSHUAH;
   THEY WILL PRAISE YOUR HOLY NAME.
FOR YOU ARE GREAT AND PERFORM WONDERFUL DEEDS.
   YOU ALONE ARE THE SOVEREIGN KING.

TEACH ME YOUR WAYS, O TENSHUAH,
   THAT I MAY LIVE ACCORDING TO YOUR TRUTH!
   GRANT ME PURITY OF HEART,
   SO THAT I MAY HONOR YOU.
WITH ALL MY HEART I WILL PRAISE YOU, O TENSHUAH
   MY SOVEREIGN KING.
   I WILL GIVE GLORY TO YOUR NAME FOREVER,
FOR YOUR LOVE FOR ME IS VERY GREAT.
   YOU HAVE RESCUED ME FROM THE DEPTHS OF DEATH.

O SOVEREIGN KING, INSOLENT PEOPLE RISE UP AGAINST ME;
   A VIOLENT GANG IS TRYING TO KILL ME.
   YOU MEAN NOTHING TO THEM.
BUT YOU, O TENSHUAH,
   ARE A GOD OF COMPASSION AND MERCY,
   SLOW TO GET ANGRY
   AND FILLED WITH UNFAILING LOVE AND FAITHFULNESS.
LOOK DOWN AND HAVE MERCY ON ME.
   GIVE YOUR STRENGTH TO YOUR SERVANT;
   SAVE ME, THE SON OF YOUR SERVANT.
SEND ME A SIGN OF YOUR FAVOR.
   THEN THOSE WHO HATE ME WILL BE PUT TO SHAME,
   FOR YOU, O TENSHUAH, HELP AND COMFORT ME.

TO BE ACCOMPANIED BY THE GUITARP

This song is based on Psalm 86 (NLT)

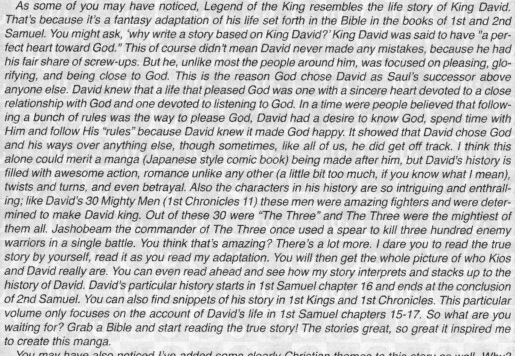

THE REAL KIOS

As some of you may have noticed, Legend of the King resembles the life story of King David. That's because it's a fantasy adaptation of his life set forth in the Bible in the books of 1st and 2nd Samuel. You might ask, 'why write a story based on King David?' King David was said to have "a perfect heart toward God." This of course didn't mean David never made any mistakes, because he had his fair share of screw-ups. But he, unlike most the people around him, was focused on pleasing, glorifying, and being close to God. This is the reason God chose David as Saul's successor above anyone else. David knew that a life that pleased God was one with a sincere heart devoted to a close relationship with God and one devoted to listening to God. In a time were people believed that following a bunch of rules was the way to please God, David had a desire to know God, spend time with Him and follow His "rules" because David knew it made God happy. It showed that David chose God and his ways over anything else, though sometimes, like all of us, he did get off track. I think this alone could merit a manga (Japanese style comic book) being made after him, but David's history is filled with awesome action, romance unlike any other (a little bit too much, if you know what I mean), twists and turns, and even betrayal. Also the characters in his history are so intriguing and enthralling; like David's 30 Mighty Men (1st Chronicles 11) these men were amazing fighters and were determined to make David king. Out of these 30 were "The Three" and The Three were the mightiest of them all. Jashobeam the commander of The Three once used a spear to kill three hundred enemy warriors in a single battle. You think that's amazing? There's a lot more. I dare you to read the true story by yourself, read it as you read my adaptation. You will then get the whole picture of who Kios and David really are. You can even read ahead and see how my story interprets and stacks up to the history of David. David's particular history starts in 1st Samuel chapter 16 and ends at the conclusion of 2nd Samuel. You can also find snippets of his story in 1st Kings and 1st Chronicles. This particular volume only focuses on the account of David's life in 1st Samuel chapters 15-17. So what are you waiting for? Grab a Bible and start reading the true story! The stories great, so great it inspired me to create this manga.

You may have also noticed I've added some clearly Christian themes to this story as well. Why? Well, first of all, Jesus is a descendant of King David, so obviously he has a lot to do with David. But, more personally, I'm a Christian and Christian ideas and ideals are important to me; but also because Jesus, and the things He taught and lived out are important for us all so that we can live a more fulfilled life, free from sin and guilt. The sacrifice of Jesus' perfect life on the cross can free us from the guilt of our sins. And if we're honest with ourselves our sins are many. When we're free from sins guilt we'll also be filled with Jesus' joy and peace (we can all use more of these things). Also the "perfect heart" David had was something that Jesus calls us to have as well. Jesus calls us to repent of our sins, trust in Him to save us, and follow his holy standards. An example of a Christian theme that I added into this comic that wasn't in David's original story is, The Golden Rule, "Do to others as you would have them do to you (Matthew 7:12, Luke 6:31)." There are some more, but I'll leave them for you to find. If you find some of them you can e-mail me at **stoaked@lotkcomic.com** with your thoughts and even where they are referenced in the New Testament. If you do, I may post your comments and my responses to them in the next volumes "The Real Kios" section.

Sincerely,

Adam Stoak

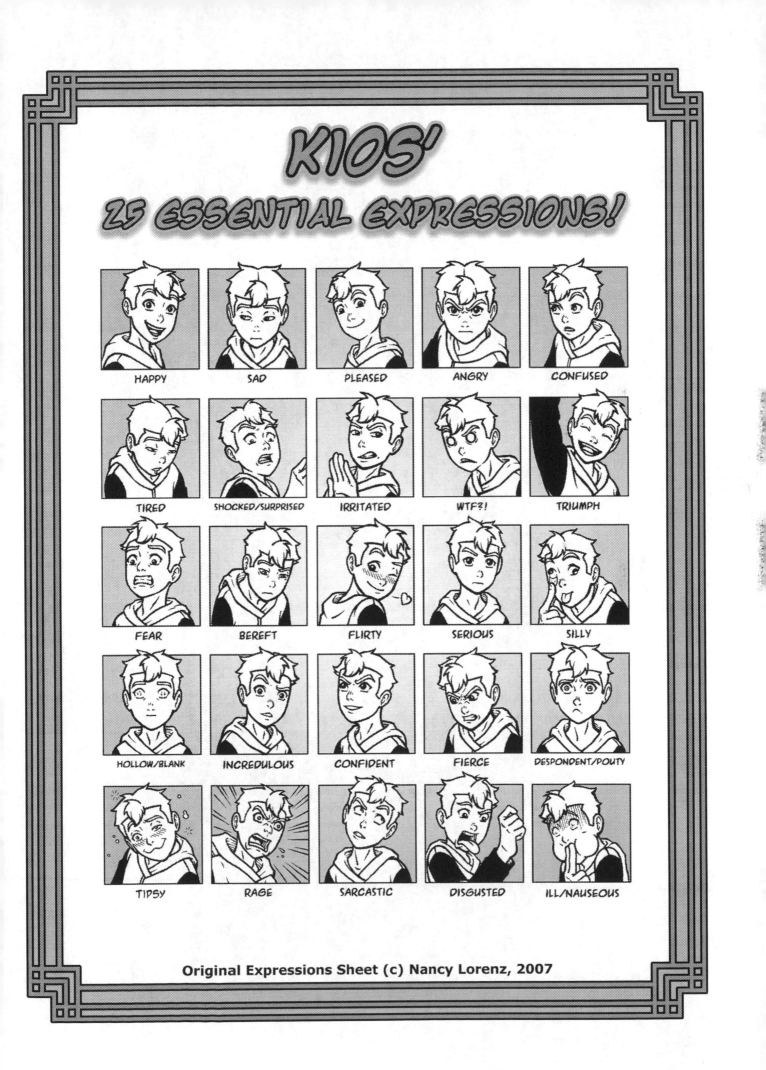

KIOS' 25 ESSENTIAL EXPRESSIONS!

HAPPY · SAD · PLEASED · ANGRY · CONFUSED

TIRED · SHOCKED/SURPRISED · IRRITATED · WTF?! · TRIUMPH

FEAR · BEREFT · FLIRTY · SERIOUS · SILLY

HOLLOW/BLANK · INCREDULOUS · CONFIDENT · FIERCE · DESPONDENT/POUTY

TIPSY · RAGE · SARCASTIC · DISGUSTED · ILL/NAUSEOUS

Original Expressions Sheet (c) Nancy Lorenz, 2007

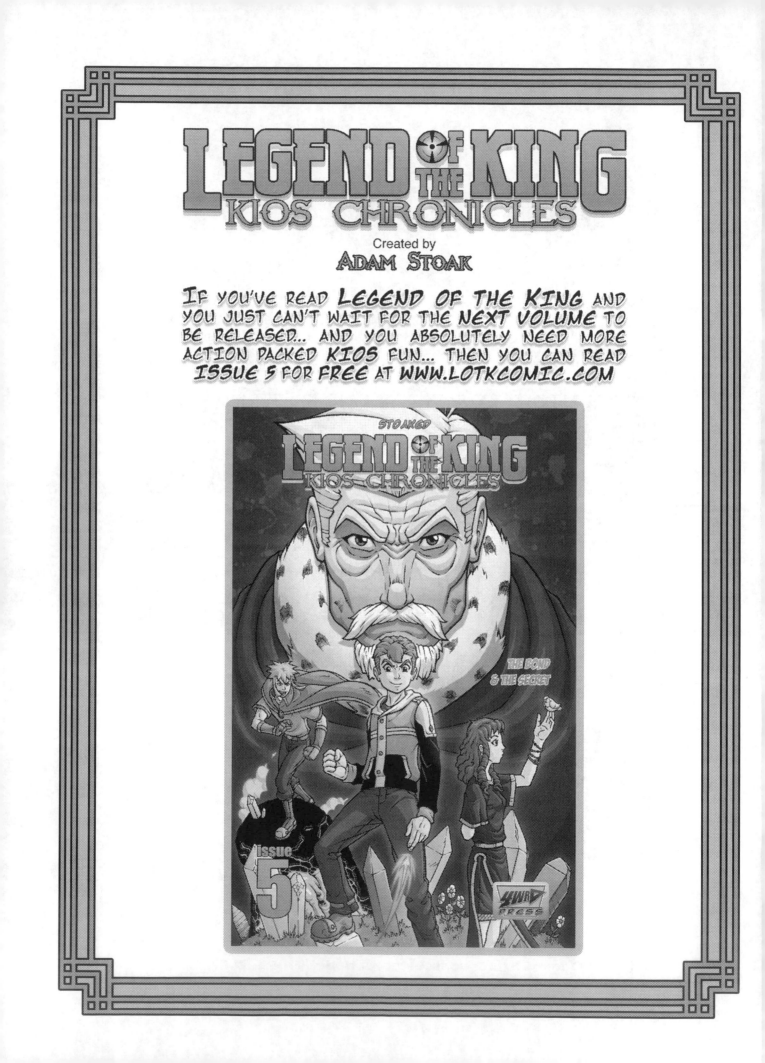

ADAM STOAK'S ART HAS BEEN PUBLISHED IN THE RPG CHAMPIONS, THE BOARD GAME KINGS OF ISRAEL, AND IN THE DIGITAL COMICS APP CLOUD 9 COMIX. IT'S BEEN HIS DREAM TO BE A PUBLISHED COMIC ARTIST SINCE HE WAS EIGHT YEARS OLD, WHEN HE READ HIS FIRST X-MEN COMIC. STOAK CURRENTLY LIVES IN HARRISBURG, PENNSYLVANIA, WITH HIS WIFE AND THEIR TWO ENERGETIC SONS.